Cakes and Miracles
A PURIM TALE

by Barbara Diamond Goldin · illustrated by Erika Weihs

VIKING

The art was painted in oils on
gessoed acid-free boards.

VIKING
Published by the Penguin Group
Viking Penguin, a division of Penguin Books USA Inc.,
375 Hudson Street, New York, New York 10014, U.S.A.
Penguin Books Ltd, 27 Wrights Lane, London W8 5TZ, England
Penguin Books Australia Ltd, Ringwood, Victoria, Australia
Penguin Books Canada Ltd, 2801 John Street, Markham, Ontario, Canada L3R 1B4
Penguin Books (N.Z.) Ltd, 182–190 Wairau Road, Auckland 10, New Zealand

Penguin Books Ltd, Registered Offices: Harmondsworth, Middlesex, England

First published in 1991 by Viking Penguin, a division of Penguin Books USA Inc.

1 3 5 7 9 10 8 6 4 2

Text copyright © Barbara Diamond Goldin, 1991
Illustrations copyright © Erika Weihs, 1991
All rights reserved

Library of Congress Cataloging-in-Publication Data
Goldin, Barbara Diamond.
Cakes and miracles : a Purim tale /
Barbara Diamond Goldin : illustrated by Erika Weihs   p.   cm.
Summary: Young, blind Hershel finds that he has special gifts he
can use to help his mother during the Jewish holiday of Purim.
I S B N 0 - 6 7 0 - 8 3 0 4 7 - X
[1. Purim—Fiction. 2. Blind—Fiction. 3. Physically
handicapped—Fiction.] I. Weihs, Erika, ill. II. Title.
PZ7.G5674Cak   1991   [E]—dc20
90-42048   CIP   AC

Printed in Japan
Set in 14 point Sabon

For my son, Jeremy Casey, who sees not only with his eyes,
but in his dreams, and shapes with his hands.

B.D.G.

In memory of Tommy,
and for Kurt, John, and Kris.

E.W.

Hershel was the only blind boy in his village. But his blindness did not keep him from going to school, or playing by the river, or shaking pears from the neighbor's tree.

"You scamp!" his mother, Basha, would say. "Don't I have enough work to do without washing the mud off your pants, or bringing cakes to Reb Shimmel, who threatens every day to kick you out of school?"

Hershel behaved in school when the boys chanted from the Bible. It was when they practiced their writing that he grew bored. That was when he would pull out a frog from his pocket and let it loose in the classroom. Oh, how he loved to hear the other boys laugh at poor Reb Shimmel, who jumped up and down and danced around the frog!

It wasn't easy to catch the frogs. Hershel spent many hours by the river waiting quietly, listening. He didn't catch every frog. But, if he waited long enough and was patient enough, he could pounce and reach in just the right place. Oh, then he was happy!

The river was Hershel's favorite place in the village. Besides frogs and water and friends, there was mud to play in. Hershel made mountains, and streams going around the mountains, with the cool, smooth mud. He could make the mud do anything he wanted it to do. A poke here and he had a cave. A push there, he had a tunnel. He tried to wash the mud off his clothes before he went home, but he always missed a patch or two.

"You have to go to the river and get all muddy?" Basha would say when he came inside. "If you had eyes, you could see all the mud on your clothes."

Hershel winced. How he hated to hear his mother say that: "If you had eyes." And he did not mean to make extra work for her. It was true. Ever since his father died, she was busy enough doing a little bit of this and a little bit of that to feed and clothe the two of them.

She sewed. She cleaned. She cooked. She baked. Especially in early spring, at Purim time, she baked. Then the three-cornered fat cakes called *hamantashen* filled with prunes or poppy seeds sold well in the marketplace.

On Purim day, back and forth, back and forth, the children carried plates filled with *hamantashen* and other treats. From this house to that house, they carried the gifts that were sweet reminders of the joyful victory of good over evil, long ago in the city of Shushan, in Persia.

"This year, maybe I can sell enough *hamantashen* to buy two more chickens, or even a milk cow," Basha said hopefully.

"This year, maybe I can help you with the cakes," said Hershel.

"This year, maybe you can fetch the water and bring in the kindling," answered Basha. "A person needs eyes to shape the dough. Now go."

"A person needs eyes. A person needs eyes," Hershel mumbled to himself as he did his chores. "Can I help it if I have eyes, but do not see?"

He carried a big stack of wood into the house.

Bang went the door behind him.

"Is this all I will do when I'm thirteen? When I'm a man? Fetch water and bring in the wood?"

Bang. He went out again.

"What will we do when Mother is too old to sew and clean, cook and bake?"

Bang. Bang.

"Enough," said Basha. "Enough, Hershel. Now go to sleep. We have a lot to do tomorrow. It's the day before Purim."

Hershel stomped off to his bed.

"And what about a good night from my son?" Basha asked softly, holding her arms out.

"Good night, Mama," he said. He gave her a peck on the cheek. How could he stay angry with a mother who cared for him so?

Hershel climbed into his bed near the stove. After he said his bedtime
prayer, the *Shema,* he added a prayer of his own. "If only I could see. If
only I could help my mother," he whispered. "Really help her."

That night, Hershel had a dream. In his dream, he saw the most beautiful
winged angel descending a sparkling ladder. The angel bent down toward
Hershel and spoke.

"Make what you see," the angel said.

Hershel protested to the angel, "But I don't see. I haven't been able to see since I was sick. The doctor from Kotsk said I will never see again."

"You see when you close your eyes. You see in your dreams," the angel answered.

"It's true. I can see in my dreams," Hershel whispered.

Hershel awoke and the angel was gone. But he remembered what the angel said.

Soon, he heard his mother stoking the stove. "Mother," he called out. "Good news! The doctor from Kotsk was wrong. I can see. In my head. And I can help you with your cakes."

"Hershel, Hershel," said Basha, shaking her head. "You wish you could see. I wish you could see. But how can a blind boy see? In his head or out of his head? I can't let you play with the cake dough. I need every *hamantashen*."

"But I won't play, Mother. I'll make cakes. Or maybe something different. Cookies. Cookies in wonderful shapes to sell."

"Not just a cookie! But shapes, too? Hershel, only I touch the dough. You help me just as you always do. Yes?"

"Yes, Mother," Hershel said sadly.

"And right after school, you come right home. No mud or funny business."

After school, Hershel did his chores. He fetched. He carried. He cleaned pans, while his mother mixed and rolled and cut and baked.

At nightfall, Basha said, "I'll leave this batch of dough to roll and cut in the morning, Purim morning." And they went to synagogue to hear the chanting of the *Megillah*, the story of Queen Esther.

Hershel did not forget his noisemaker. Every child had one. Some were made of wood and as big as kitchen tables. Some were just two rocks to hit together or a shoe to bang on the floor. And every time the Rabbi chanted the name of the villain, Haman, his voice was drowned by the shaking, rattling, bellowing, and stamping. What fun Hershel had.

But during the night, when everyone slept, tired from noisemaking and revelry, Hershel could not sleep.

It was as if the angel were repeating over and over again in Hershel's ears, "You see in your dreams. Make what you see."

Hershel sat up. He was drawn to the kitchen where his mother's *ha-mantashen* lay, ready to bring to market.

He felt for the bowl filled with dough and took a piece with his hands. The cool smoothness of it made him think of the mud by the river. But instead of mountains and streams, he would make little cookies to sell.

Hershel kneaded the dough. Then he formed a bird and a fish and a goblet. As he worked, he found it easier and easier to shape the cookies so they matched the images dancing in his head.

As the night turned to day, his mother awoke.

"What are you doing, Hershel?" she demanded. "I told you not to play with the dough. You will ruin it."

Then she saw Hershel's cookies.

"But . . . but . . . they are beautiful, Hershel. A wonder. How can a boy who cannot see make such . . ."

"But I can see," Hershel interrupted. "When I close my eyes, I see."

"Truly a miracle!" Basha said, and took Hershel's face tenderly in her hands.

"Do you think people will buy them, Mother?" worried Hershel.

"Do onions grow in the ground?" Basha answered. "But we won't sell even one standing here in the kitchen. I'll bake your cookies and we'll carry them all to market."

The market was already a busy place, even busier than usual. Hershel could smell the familiar odor of herring and pickles, bread and cheeses. He could hear the chickens cackling and the vendors calling out. But today there were new, sweet smells coming from the tables loaded with Purim treats: the honey cakes, the bottles of syrups, pears, wines, the *hamantashen* shaped like Haman's three-cornered hat. Happy sounds, laughing sounds, teasing and joking sounds floated around, in and out and over the chickens' cackles and the vendors' calls.

Hershel and Basha set out their baked goods.

"Buy a special cake for Purim!" Basha called. "A delicious *haman-tashen* fat with filling. Or a cookie in the shape of the horse that Mordecai rode through Shushan. Honor Queen Esther, who saved our people from the wicked Haman.

"Perhaps your friend would like a little bird for her Purim gift? Have you ever seen one so beautiful?" Basha said to a young girl, who looked from the bird to the flower to the horse.

Soon there was quite a crowd around Basha's table.

"Basha," said Hava the midwife, "what fine cakes and cookies you have this year. I have never seen you make such flowers or fish."

"My son made them," Basha said proudly. "My son who can see with his hands."

"Blind Hershel?" Hava exclaimed in disbelief. "A miracle! Like something from heaven. I will buy that one. And that one, too."

Fayge the belt maker wanted four cookies. And Lieba the feather picker wanted three. Even Berel the baker bought a cookie, the last one. He pinched Hershel's cheek as he walked by.

"You'll be a talented baker some day," he said. "Come talk to me."

"Hershel." His mother turned to him. "Did you hear what Berel said? You're a talent. It's not every day a nice word like that comes from his mouth. And every *hamantashen*, every cookie is gone."

"It's true, Mother?" Hershel asked. "Every one sold?"

Hershel couldn't see the table. But he could feel the excitement all around him. Purim excitement. Cookie excitement. Talent excitement. And in his head, he could see himself as a man, a baker perhaps, with bowls of flour all around. Or a carpenter, or a shoemaker, or a toolmaker.

Oh, how happy Hershel was. Suddenly the words of a Purim song jumped into his head and he couldn't shake them out. They danced around inside until Hershel was singing them right out loud.

"What a happy holiday,
What a happy holiday!
We dance and sing,
And make some noise,
And eat our hamantashen."

Picking up the tune again, Hershel added, *"And a cookie!"*

ABOUT THIS BOOK

Purim, one of the noisiest and most enjoyable of all the Jewish holidays, occurs on the fourteenth day of the Hebrew month of Adar (February or March). The story of Purim, found in the biblical book of Esther, is an exciting account of court intrigue, life and death struggles, and victory for the underdog.

The setting is ancient Persia. The king, Ahasuerus, has recently chosen a new queen, Esther. She is an orphan who has been raised by her cousin, Mordecai.

Trouble for the Jews begins when Haman, the highest court official, realizes that Mordecai will not bow down to him. In anger, he plots to kill all the Jews of Persia. The king, who is unaware that Esther is Jewish, grants Haman permission to destroy her people. The word "Purim" comes from the Hebrew word, *pur,* which means "lot," referring to the lots Haman cast to select the date of destruction.

When Mordecai learns of the royal decree, he sends word to Esther. Since no one is allowed to call upon the king unless summoned, Esther risks her life when she enters the inner court to speak to Ahasuerus. She finds favor with the king and informs him

of Haman's intention to kill her people. The tables are turned: the king orders that Haman suffer the fate he had planned for Mordecai and the Jews.

Turning the tables is the order of the day for Purim. People dress up in costume, perform skits and parodies, eat, drink, and sing. When the *Megillah,* the story of Esther, is chanted in the synagogue, there is booing and hissing whenever Haman's name is mentioned. Traditional noisemakers, called *graggers,* and nontraditional ones, such as horns and whistles, add to the din.

On this joyous holiday, Jews give charity and gifts to the poor. Gifts for friends and relatives are called *mishloah manot* and consist of ready-to-eat food. They often include the traditional *hamantashen,* the triangular pastries filled with fruit or poppy seeds that resemble Haman's three-cornered hat.

In these ways, Jews all over the world from then until now have observed the day that was transformed from one of grief and mourning to one of "light and gladness, happiness and honor" (Esther 8:16). Masks, tricks, noise, and turning tables mark Purim, a grand celebration.

Make Your Own *Hamantashen*

Eating plenty of *hamantashen* is part of the fun of Purim. Some people say this three-cornered pastry reminds us of the evil court advisor, Haman—of his hat, his pockets, or his ears.

The word *"hamantashen"* comes from two German or Yiddish words. *Mohn* means poppyseeds and *tashen* means pockets. As the pastry became associated with Purim, the word changed to *hamantashen.*

Traditionally, *hamantashen* were filled with a poppyseed mixture; later a prune filling became common. But today, we can delight in filling these pockets with whatever mixture tastes good and adds to the joy of the holiday.

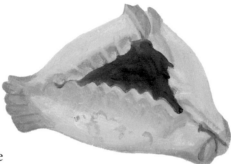

For the **dough** you will need:
4 cups all-purpose flour
1 cup sugar
3 teaspoons baking powder
½ teaspoon salt
3 large eggs, beaten
4 tablespoons orange juice
1 cup margarine or butter,
   softened to room temperature

For the **filling** you will need:
3 ounces cream cheese, softened
2 teaspoons jam (any flavor)
¼ cup chopped nuts

An alternate can be strawberry, apricot, prune, or other preserves. Children enjoy a filling of 4 or 5 chocolate chips, or a dab of peanut butter and a dab of jelly.

1. Preheat oven to 350°. Grease two cookie sheets.
2. Using an electric mixer, cream the margarine and sugar together in a large bowl.
3. Add the eggs and orange juice. Mix well.
4. In a separate bowl, mix together the flour, baking powder, and salt. Add the flour mixture to the sugar and egg mixture. Mix together with a large spoon. If this mixture is too sticky, add a little more flour. (The dough will be easier to handle if you refrigerate it for an hour or more.)
5. Since the dough will be soft, sprinkle flour on the rolling pin and on a piece of waxed paper that you use to roll out the dough—so it doesn't stick. Roll out the dough to ⅛–¼ inch thickness.
6. Find a round glass, mug, or cookie cutter with a rim about 2½–3 inches across. Flour the rim. Use it to cut the dough into circles.
7. Mix together the filling ingredients. Put about ¾ of a teaspoon of filling in the center of each circle. Shape into triangles by bringing two sides of the circle up to the center and pinching them together. Then bring up the third side and pinch it to the other two sides. Be sure to pinch the dough firmly so the pastry will not open during the baking. Do not close the tops completely, so some filling shows in the center.
8. Place the *hamantashen* on the greased cookie sheets, about an inch apart. Bake for 10–12 minutes until lightly browned along the edges. Cool on wire racks. Makes about 5 dozen.